Disney's THE LION KING SHORT STORIES

Disney's

THE LION KING

SHORT STORIES

Written by Nigel Robinson

Scholastic Children's Books
Commonwealth House, 1–19 New Oxford Street,
London WC1A 1NU, UK
a division of Scholastic Ltd
London ~ New York ~ Toronto ~ Sydney ~ Auckland

First published in the UK by Scholastic Ltd, 1997

Text by Nigel Robinson

ISBN 0 590 19046 6

Typeset by TW Typesetting, Midsomer Norton, Somerset
Printed by Cox & Wyman Ltd, Reading, Berks.
10 9 8 7 6 5 4 3 2 1

1

Zebra Crossing

In the days when Simba was still a lion cub, he and his best friend, Nala, loved to play with all the other creatures living in the Pride Lands. One of their greatest friends was Punda, a young zebra.

Simba, Nala and Punda went everywhere together. They played hide-and-seek in the bush, and Punda always lost. That wasn't really Punda's fault. With his distinctive black-and-white striped coat it was hard for him to hide anywhere. On the other hand, Simba and Nala's golden fur blended in perfectly with the browns and golds of the bushes and thorn trees.

The three of them also raced each other across the wide open plains. Punda usually won this game. His legs were strong and muscular and made for running. Simba and Nala, however, were still very small, and soon they would be out of breath and have to give up their game.

"We're great pals, aren't we?" Simba asked Punda one day, after they had stopped playing to drink at a nearby water hole.

They were all hot and very thirsty.

"The best," Punda agreed. He sipped at the water. It was a little muddy, but, in the heat of the afternoon sun, it tasted wonderful.

"And we'll always be friends?" Simba continued. "Forever and ever and ever?"

Punda nodded. He stopped drinking, to allow Nala to drink some water, and looked over into the distance.

Standing on the crest of a small hill was his mother, Milia. She looked proud and graceful, even as she swung her long black tail from side to side, to swat away the flies.

Standing next to her was the wildebeest, Nyumbu. They made a very odd couple. Milia was slender, whereas Nyumbu was cumbersome and ungainly, with rolls of fat, a long scraggly beard and two enormous curved horns. However, he was an old friend of Punda's family, and he had always been very kind to Punda.

Punda turned to his two friends. "I have to go now," he told them sadly.

"Oh, you're no fun!" Simba said. "Can't your mum let you play with us for a little bit longer?"

Punda shook his head.

"You won't know unless you ask her!" Simba protested.

"I don't need to ask," Punda said mysteriously. "When Nyumbu is with my mother then I know that it's time to go..."

Nala looked strangely at Punda. There was a strange note of sadness in the young zebra's voice.

"Will we see you tomorrow?" she asked.

Punda seemed uncertain. "I don't know," he replied.

"We'll meet you by the big baobab tree," Simba decided. "When the sun is high in the sky. OK?"

Punda said that he'd try to meet his friends by the tree tomorrow, and then he galloped off to join his mother and Nyumbu.

After he had left, Nala turned to Simba.

"I think he's really creepy," she said.

"Who? Punda?" Simba asked.

"No, silly," Nala replied. "Nyumbu."

"Wildebeest are like that," Simba said knowledgeably. "All grumpy and silent. My dad says that's because they think too much and so they don't have time to talk."

"I wonder what he's thinking of?" Nala said. "Whatever it is, I bet it's important for him to look so serious."

"Who cares?" Simba said, and then added, "You know something, Nala? I don't think Punda's mum likes us."

"Why do you say that?" Nala asked.

"Well, when you and me are grown up, then we'll have to hunt zebra," Simba told her.

"I know," Nala said. She thought for a moment and then added, "I don't think I want to grow up."

"It's OK though," Simba said. "My dad told me all about it. We kill the zebra, and then, when we die, our bodies help the grass to grow. And the zebra and the antelope and the wildebeest all feed on the grass. My dad calls it the Circle of Life."

"It's all very complicated," Nala said.

"Well, it's natural – it's what we're meant to do!" Simba replied. "But whatever happens Punda will always be our pal. You, me and Punda are going to be friends for a long, long time!"

"Where is he?" Simba asked the following day. He and Nala had been waiting for Punda at the foot of the big baobab tree.

Simba looked up into the sky. The sun was directly overhead now, and still Punda hadn't turned up.

"Maybe he's been held up?" Nala suggested.

"Or maybe his mum has told him that he can't see us any more," Simba thought.

"Maybe he's been kidnapped or something. That would be exciting, wouldn't it?"

"No, it wouldn't," Nala replied. She was beginning to get very worried indeed.

"Maybe he's forgotten," Simba suggested.

"But Punda's our friend," Nala said sadly. "He wouldn't let us down like this, would he?"

Just at that moment, Simba's Uncle Scar

walked by. Scar was the brother of Simba's father, King Mufasa. He had been second-in-line to the throne until Simba was born. Now Scar hated Simba and was forever thinking of ways to get rid of him.

"Hi, Uncle Scar!" Simba said, and ran up to the older lion. "How're you doing?"

"'How're you doing?'" Scar repeated, in a voice too low for Simba to hear. "What sort of greeting is that to the King's own brother? What do they teach these irritating pretenders to the throne nowadays?"

Scar smiled insincerely. "Well, hello, my dearest nephew," he said. "I am 'doing' very well indeed. But what are *you* doing out here?" He looked up at the sun. "Here in the blazing noon-day sun. Why, in this frightful heat you might even fry to death."

("I'd even provide the frying pan myself," Scar thought evilly.) "We're waiting for our friend, Punda," Simba said, and told Scar all about the zebra.

"But he's late," Nala added. "We're getting a little worried about him."

"You don't think anything's happened to him, do you, Uncle Scar?" Simba asked.

Scar pretended to think about it. "You say that he's never been late before?" he asked.

"That's right," Simba replied, and then exchanged a look with Nala. "I bet it's all the fault of that wildebeest after all!"

Scar sighed. "Well, there is one other possibility..." he began, and then shook his head.

"But it's too terrible even to contemplate..."

Simba felt his heart sink. "What is it, Uncle Scar?" he asked.

"No, no, no. It's too much for your sensitive souls to bear," he said slyly, and wiped a big tear from out of the corner of his eye.

"Uncle Scar, we *have* to know," Simba said firmly. "If Punda is in danger then we have to go and help him! He's our friend."

"No, I can't tell you..."

"*Please.*"

"Oh, very well then," Scar said finally. "I've heard rumours that hyenas have been seen in the Pride Lands again."

"Hyenas!" said Simba and Nala at the same time.

They all knew what that meant. Hyenas were the most vicious killers of them all, and would even snatch new-born babies from their mothers. Hyenas were some of the most evil creatures in the whole of Africa.

"Of course, it could be just a rumour," Scar said. "But if your young friend has wandered off on his own, well, then I shudder to think of the consequences..."

Scar didn't have to say anything more. Both

Simba and Nala knew what would happen to Punda if he was attacked by a pack of hungry hyenas.

"We must save him!" Nala said.

"Where have the hyenas been seen, Uncle Scar?" Simba asked urgently.

"I don't really know if I should tell you," Scar replied.

Simba tugged at his evil uncle's mane. "You must tell us, Uncle Scar, you must! Punda is our friend – we must rescue him!"

"Well, if you insist," Scar said. "But you must promise not to let your father know that I told you this. Promise?"

"We promise," Simba said. "But hurry up! Punda could be in terrible danger!"

Scar pointed to a dot just on the horizon, at the very edge of the Pride Lands.

"They say that the hyenas have been seen there," he told them. "But please don't go after them, Simba. It's far, far too dangerous."

"We must," Simba cried. "Punda is our friend. And you should never let your friends down. Let's go, Nala!"

Simba and Nala raced off in the direction his uncle had indicated. As soon as they had gone,

Scar sniggered.

Scar knew that there were no hyenas there. But there soon would be.

He'd make sure of that.

"I don't like this place at all, Simba," Nala said.

They had arrived in a deep gully, surrounded on all sides by tall trees which cut out much of the sun's light. A few ash-coloured skulls lay on the ground and swarms of flies buzzed around them. Nearby, there stood several termite mounds, each of which was four or five feet high.

"This is where Punda must be," Simba said, although he wasn't quite so sure any more.

"But why would he come here?" Nala asked. "It's an awful place."

Simba had to agree. The ground was cracked and dry, with no sign of the lush and green vegetation that their zebra friend loved to eat.

Perhaps they had been wrong and Punda hadn't been captured by hyenas, after all. Perhaps he'd just forgotten their date. But that was so unlike Punda – he never forgot anything and he could even beat the elephants at their memory games.

"Simba, let's go home," Nala said.

"OK," Simba said. "There doesn't seem to be much here for us."

He turned to go and then gulped. A pair of evil-looking faces had popped out from behind a termite mound and were staring down at him. They had long snouts and cruel eyes. What was more, they had the sharpest teeth Simba had ever seen in his life.

"Leaving so soon?" cackled one of the hyenas,

and licked his lips. "Why don't you both stay for dinner?"

Simba tried to run, but the other hyena grabbed his tail. Simba fell flat on his face in the dust.

"Run, Nala!" Simba shouted to his companion.

"I can't leave without you!" she cried.

"Save yourself!"

Nala ran off. For a moment, the second hyena thought about following her and then changed his mind. Running after Nala seemed too much like hard work and hyenas were pretty lazy. He turned back to his fellow hyena, who was dangling Simba by the tail, playing with him like a cat teasing a mouse.

"Leave me alone, you bullies!" Simba said and tried to punch the hyena.

He just laughed. "And why should we do that?" he asked.

"If you don't then my father, the King, will come and get you!"

"Oooh, and aren't we scared!" the hyenas laughed sarcastically. "So you're Mufasa's little brat Simba then, are you? It looks like we're in for a right royal banquet!"

Simba trembled. He was helpless. It looked like this was the end.

Nala ran as fast as she could across the plain. She had to get help for Simba, and she knew that the zebra could help her. They were some of the fastest runners in the Pride Lands, and they'd be able to reach King Mufasa much quicker than she could.

However, when she looked around she couldn't see anyone. It was very strange, she thought. Normally the grasslands were full of zebra and wildebeest but today they all seemed to have disappeared. Where had they all gone?

Her heart leapt as she looked up, and recognized a flash of blue flying past in the sky.

"Zazu!" she cried. The hornbill heard her cry and flew down.

"Nala, what are you doing here, so far away from Pride Rock?" he asked.

"No time to explain," she panted. "Simba, back there—" She nodded towards the gully.

"That little scamp," Zazu tut-tutted. "How often have I told him about straying away from home—"

"Hyenas!"

"Hyenas!" Zazu shot into the air; even the name gave him palpitations.

"Tell King Mufasa!" Nala begged. "Before it's too late!"

"At once!" Zazu replied, and started to fly back to Pride Rock.

The hyenas snapped at Simba with their long sharp fangs. They were only teasing him so far, Simba realized. However, when they had tired of their little game then ... well, Simba didn't really want to think about what would happen then. He just hoped that it would be over quickly.

"You won't get away with this!" he told them. "My father will come and rescue me. And so will my Uncle Scar."

For some reason the mention of Scar's name made the hyenas laugh even more.

What Simba didn't know was that it was Scar who had sent the hyenas to capture him. He'd passed the message on through the vultures, promising them that they could have what was left of Simba after the hyenas had finished with him.

One of the hyenas yawned. "I'm getting hungry," he said. The other hyena grinned.

"Okey-dokey," he said. "Dinner is served!"

Suddenly there was an earth-shattering roar and Mufasa leapt into the gully, followed by Zazu. He swiped at the two hyenas with his mighty claws and they were forced to drop Simba.

Simba ran over to Zazu, and watched as his dad chased the two hyenas away. They raced off, trailing a cloud of dust behind them.

Mufasa didn't bother to give chase, but instead turned to his son. "Simba, are you all right?" he asked anxiously.

"Of course I am," Simba replied, and dusted himself down. "I was only fooling them. I could have taken them all out at one go if I'd wanted to!"

Mufasa laughed. "Of course you could, my son," he said affectionately. "Of course you could."

Just then Nala arrived. She sighed with relief when she saw that Simba was safe.

"But what were you two doing here in the first place?" Mufasa asked them.

"We were looking for our friend, Punda," Simba told him. "He's gone missing, and we thought that the hyenas had got him."

"Gone missing?" Mufasa asked, and then smiled. "I think I can tell you where Punda has gone. Follow me."

Simba, Nala and Zazu followed Mufasa as he

led them across the plain. Like Nala, Simba also noticed that there were very few zebra or wildebeest grazing here. Mufasa led them all to the top of a ridge and told them to look down into the valley below.

"Wow!" said Simba.

Below them thousands of zebra and wildebeest were crossing over the plain, marching out of the Pride Lands, and heading south. It was one of the most amazing sights Simba had ever seen in his life.

"What is it, Dad?" he asked.

"The annual migration of the zebra and wildebeest," Mufasa told him. "It has rained down in the southlands, and there is plenty of green grass there for them to eat."

"And Punda is down there with them?" Nala asked.

Mufasa nodded his head. "Punda is there, as well as Milia and Nyumbu," he said.

Simba sighed. "I suppose this means that we'll never see them again?" he asked his father.

"They will come back again, when the time is right," Mufasa said. "It's all part of the natural order of things."

"Punda was a good pal," Simba said. "I'll miss him."

"Me too," agreed Nala.

"Absence will make your heart grow fonder," Mufasa said. "And no matter how far away from you he is, Punda will still be your friend, and one day he will return. That's what friendship is, Simba. And Simba..."

"Yes, Dad?"

"I am proud of you," Mufasa said. "You were very brave."

"Punda is my friend," Simba replied. "I had to help him – even though he wasn't really in any danger. After all, he's a pal. And you should never let your pals down, should you, Dad?"

"That's right, Simba – you should never let your friends down," Mufasa agreed. "Now come along, Simba, your mother is waiting for you..."

2

And on the Menu Tonight...

In the days before Simba became the Lion King, he lived with the tiny meerkat Timon, and the fat warthog, Pumbaa, in the forests and jungles far from the Pride Lands. He had fled there when he believed that he was directly responsible for the death of his father, King Mufasa.

In the meantime, the real murderer, Simba's evil Uncle Scar, had assumed the throne of the Pride Lands, and was ruling over a land of fear, with the help of his hyena shock troops.

Simba, Timon and Pumbaa got on very well together. They'd spend most of the days searching for the juicy and succulent grubs which lay under stones and logs and branches. They'd spend the evenings playing games or talking and telling stories to each other late into the night.

Often they would wonder about the tiny pricks

of light twinkling up above them in the night sky. The three of them could never quite agree on what the stars were. Timon said that they were fireflies, while Pumbaa was of the firm opinion that they were big balls of gas millions and millions of miles away.

Simba, on the other hand, remembered his father once telling him that the stars in the sky were really the spirits of the great kings of the past. Mufasa had said that their spirits were always looking down on Simba, ready to guide him whenever he needed their help.

Like all good friends, Simba, Timon and Pumbaa would sometimes have arguments and fall out with each other. However, they always made up in the end.

Timon and Pumbaa were having an argument now. They'd both shared a pair of tasty cater-pillars for lunch, and now they had their hungry eyes on a particularly juicy-looking giant millipede. It was at least fifteen inches long, which was large even for a millipede, and it was just the thing to share for their evening meal.

Timon had wanted to capture the bug, but he was feeling sluggish, as he had already eaten far too much. So Pumbaa volunteered to chase the

millipede. However, as soon as he approached the creature, it had raced away as fast as its hundreds of tiny little legs could carry it. It had hidden itself under a heavy stone, which not even Timon could lift and had started laughing at him.

"You fool!" Timon said, after Pumbaa had failed to capture the millipede. "How could you lose our dinner like that!"

"It wasn't my fault," Pumbaa said sulkily. "He heard me coming."

The meerkat slapped his forehead in despair. "Are you surprised?" he asked. "A great lumbering thing like you! They probably heard you all the way back in the Pride Lands!"

"Oh, don't be mad with me, Timon," Pumbaa pleaded.

" 'Mad' he says!" Timon said. "Our dinner runs away and he asks me not to be mad!"

"I didn't see you stepping in to help, Timon," Pumbaa pointed out.

"That's because I thought a little exercise would do you good!" Timon said. "You are getting awfully fat, you know, Pumbaa!"

Timon knew he had gone too far when he saw Pumbaa shed a tiny tear. "I can't help it," he said. "When did you ever see a thin warthog? We're supposed to be fat!"

"Whereas I am just a poor thin meerkat starving in the forest!" Timon exclaimed.

"Don't worry, Timon," Pumbaa said. "I'll catch you some dinner. Maybe I'll find a nice ants' nest, or track down a crunchy beetle for you."

"No way!" Timon said. "I'll probably have to wait for the next rains before you bring home my dinner. I'm going off to get my own – without you!" Timon headed off in one direction.

"Suit yourself!" Pumbaa replied, and headed off in the opposite direction. "Let's see which of us gets the most food!"

Simba sighed as his two friends disappeared into the forest. He supposed he'd better follow them. Otherwise, who could tell what sort of trouble they'd get themselves into?

The only problem was: who should he follow? Timon or Pumbaa.

It was getting very dark now, and, as Timon wandered through the forest, he started to realize that he was lost. All the trees looked the same, and he kept tripping over the creepers which lined this part of the forest floor.

Strange creatures called out to each other in the blackness, and Timon shuddered. It was getting really scary now, and he wondered what beasts might be hiding in the shadows, just waiting to pounce on him.

Timon knew that Pumbaa would have been able to frighten away any predators with his sharp and vicious-looking tusks. That was one of the reasons why they had always made a good team: Timon was the brains of the operation, and Pumbaa was the brawn. Timon wished that Pumbaa was with him now. He started to regret having been so grumpy with him earlier.

The meerkat was getting tired now, and he sat

down on a long thick log which lay on the forest floor. The log felt curiously cold and clammy to the touch, and there was a strange mottled design on its bark.

Timon thought that was odd. He thought it even odder when the log started speaking to him.

"I sssssay," the log said, "would you kindly dessssissssst from sssssitting on me?"

"Sorry," Timon said, and then looked at the log. Only it wasn't a log at all. It was a massively long python!

"Yikes!" Timon cried out, and jumped to his feet. "Er, no offence."

"And none taken, I'm sssssure," the python said and smiled a greedy smile at Timon. Its long forked tongue flicked in and out between its mighty fangs.

"Won't you ssssstay for ssssssupper?" the python asked pleasantly. It was obvious from the look in its eyes just what was on the menu.

Timon gulped. He'd seen pythons swallow a whole gazelle before, and Timon was *considerably* smaller than a gazelle.

"Er, if it's all the same to you then I'd rather not," Timon replied.

"Oh, but I musssst inssssissssst," the python said, and slithered towards the terrified Timon. The python opened its jaws wide.

"Oh, Pumbaa, big buddy, where are you now that I really need you!" Timon exclaimed, and turned and ran off through the forest with the hungry python in hot pursuit.

Pumbaa was having similar problems of his own. He'd been chasing a swarm of fireflies when he'd got hopelessly lost himself. He found himself in a part of the forest that he'd never seen before. All around him the tall trees creaked to and fro. It was certainly the spookiest place he'd ever visited in his life.

If Timon had been with him now, Pumbaa knew that the meerkat would have put his mind at rest. Those creepy noises he was hearing were only the rustling of the leaves in the branches of the trees, Timon would have told him.

And as for those two pairs of red eyes which were peering at him through the darkness, well, they were fireflies, weren't they? They certainly weren't two hungry wild dogs.

Were they?

Unfortunately for Pumbaa they were. They leapt out of the undergrowth and lunged for his throat. The warthog tried to spear them with his sharp tusks, but the dogs were too quick and nimble for him. They ducked and dived, avoiding Pumbaa's tusks by inches.

"He's much too fat and clumsy to avoid us for long, isn't he, Mwitu?" one of the dogs said to his partner. "He should go on a diet!"

"Nah – fat and clumsy – that's just the way I like 'em, Mbwa!" Mwitu cackled. "Shall we kill him now, or shall we have some fun first?"

Mbwa stopped to think. He hadn't performed

a good spot of torture since he'd come across that mongoose last week. On the other hand, he hadn't eaten since he'd tracked down an antelope yesterday, and his stomach was rumbling louder than the Maji Falls.

"We'll kill him now!" Mbwa told Mwitu, and turned to look at Pumbaa. But Pumbaa had taken advantage of the dogs' hesitation, and was already running off the way he had come.

"There goes dinner, Mbwa!" Mwitu cried.

"Let's get him!" Mbwa said and raced on after Pumbaa.

Timon ran until his legs ached and his lungs were fit to burst. The python was surprisingly quick, and seemed to know every twist and turn of the forest floor as it slithered after its prey.

"Sssstop!" the python hissed. "You know you can't esssscape me forever!"

Timon ignored the snake's taunts and continued running. He glanced behind him; the python was rapidly gaining on him.

He knew that if he didn't find some sort of hiding place soon then it would be curtains for this meerkat.

Crash!

So concerned had Timon been with the snake that he hadn't been looking where he was going. He'd ran into someone coming in the opposite direction.

"Pumbaa!" he said as he recognized his old friend. He wrapped his tiny arms around the warthog. "Oh, Pumbaa, I'm so glad to see you again!"

"Are you sure?" Pumbaa asked. He pointed at the two wild dogs which were following him.

Timon and Pumbaa clung on to each other in

fear. It looked like this was it. They were surrounded by the python on one side and the dogs on the other.

The python spat at the dogs. "Sssstay away and leave them alone!" he ordered. "I sssssaw them firsssssst!"

Mbwa and Mwitu laughed. "You think we care about that, snake-eyes?" they laughed. "They're *our* dinner!"

"Now look, guys, don't be hasty about this," Timon urged. "I'm sure that we can all come to some sort of amicable arrangement!"

"I don't disssscussss my affairs with common canines!" the python declared pompously.

"Oh yeah? Well, we'll see about that!" Mbwa and Mwitu snarled.

They leapt on to the python and began to tear at its body. The python twisted and writhed and snapped at the dogs with its fangs.

Timon and Pumbaa didn't waste a second. "C'mon, Pumbaa, run!" Timon said.

"Shouldn't we wait to see who wins?" Pumbaa asked. "After all, it's not polite to leave before dinnertime."

"Come on!" Timon sighed, and dragged Pumbaa after him.

The python and the dogs stopped their fighting.

"They're getting away!" growled Mbwa.

"After them!" hissed the python.

"Uh-oh!" said Timon and he and Pumbaa raced into the undergrowth. "Here we go again!"

Suddenly a great golden shape sprang out from behind a tree, and roared. Timon and Pumbaa heaved a sigh of relief. Simba had finally tracked them down!

The python and Mbwa and Mwitu stopped in their tracks. Their faces fell, as Simba roared at them once more. None of them had any idea what such a fierce lion was doing in the forest. However, as soon as they saw Simba's vicious teeth which were bared at them they decided that it didn't really matter.

"Heh, heh, just our little joke," Mbwa said.

"We didn't mean any harm," Mwitu claimed.

"Sssssssure, it was jussssst a game," the python said, and slunk back into the forest. Mbwa and Mwitu followed him, their tails between their legs.

When the villains had disappeared, Timon and Pumbaa hugged and thanked Simba. He'd saved their lives, and they both apologized for being foolish and going off on their own. They were a team, Timon, Pumbaa and Simba, and a team should always stick together.

"We're not out of the woods yet," Simba said.

"Course we're not," Pumbaa said. "We live in the woods. Who'd want to get out of them?"

"We're lost," Simba said. "Now does anyone know the way home?"

After about an hour of wandering through the forest, Simba, Timon and Pumbaa were still lost, and they could find no landmark which might point them on the right way home.

Even the other animals of the jungle couldn't help them.

"I'll need advance notice of that question," a prim and proper secretary bird told them when they asked her the way to go home. "I've got a very busy schedule, you know."

"Please," Pumbaa said, and looked appealingly at the bird.

"Well, I could file you under matters pending," she said graciously.

"And we could give your

address to our mates Mbwa and Mwitu," Timon had added threateningly.

That had focused the bird's mind wonderfully. "Well, it's about two miles north-west as the crow flies," she had said. "Mind you, you're not crows, are you!"

Timon and Pumbaa started to move off in two opposite directions, until Simba stopped them.

"This way is north-west," he chuckled, and led them off.

However, after two hours' walking they were still no nearer to finding their way home. Timon sat down on a log having first checked that it wasn't a python.

"Let's face facts, we're lost for ever," he said. "We'll never find the way home tonight."

"Don't be downhearted, Timon," Pumbaa said. "We'll be safe here till daylight."

"Safe he says," Timon said. "We've already been set upon by a python and two wild dogs. What next? Hyenas? Jackals? Vultures?"

"Quiet, you two," Simba said and he drew their attentions to the sky overhead.

"So what?" Timon said.

"Look," Simba said, and pointed to one of the stars. Unlike the others this one was moving.

"Let's follow that star," Simba suggested.

"Following an overgrown firefly! What next?" Timon complained, but nevertheless did as he was told. He stood up and together with Simba and Pumbaa started to walk off in the direction of the shooting star.

Sure enough, in a few minutes they were home again.

"Wow, Simba," Pumbaa said. "You're so clever!"

"How did you know?" asked Timon, who was just as impressed as Pumbaa.

Simba gazed back up into the night sky, up at the spirits of all his ancestors, of all the Lion Kings who had ever lived. It looked like King Mufasa had been right after all.

"It was just something someone told me a long, long time ago…" Simba said and smiled.

3

Rhino Trouble

Zazu seared over the Pride Lands as fast as his wings could carry him. He had important news for King Simba, and he knew that if he didn't deliver it soon, then the whole of the Pride Lands could be in mortal danger.

He spotted Simba, who was taking an afternoon nap in the shade of an acacia tree. He was alone, because Nala and all the other lionesses had gone off hunting for food. They wouldn't be back until dusk.

As Zazu flew down to greet the Lion King, Simba let out an enormous yawn, which sent the tiny hornbill reeling like a leaf caught up in a gale. He landed in an undignified heap in front of Simba. He kicked up some dust, which made Simba sneeze, and Zazu fell over once again.

"Good afternoon, Zazu," Simba chuckled,

when Zazu managed to stand up and recover his dignity. "What is it now?"

Zazu bowed low to the ground. "Sire, I bring you the most terrible and tragic news!"

"Really?" Simba asked, not very interested. The sun was high over the wide savannah, he had eaten well, and all he really wanted to do was to enjoy his well-earned doze.

However, being the Lion King Simba had certain responsibilities. Simba supposed that he had to listen to what Zazu had to say. He urged Zazu to continue.

"The antelopes are agitating, the wildebeest are

worried, and, as for the giraffes, well, they're getting to be a pain in the neck about the whole affair!" Zazu announced.

"Do get to the point, Zazu," Simba said wearily, and yawned again. Zazu did have a tendency to circle around a subject several times before coming to the point. That's what comes from being a bird, Simba supposed.

"An awful horned horror near the banks of Kifo River about a mile from here," Zazu exclaimed. "I tell you, Sire, I saw him myself and I wouldn't want to meet him alone at night in a dark Rift Valley!"

Simba chuckled. "You just saw a rhinoceros, Zazu," he said. "There's nothing to worry about."

"Nothing to worry about?" Zazu spluttered. "Nothing to worry about? Sire, an uglier and more evil-looking brute you've never seen – well, not since that despicable Scar anyway."

"We should never judge just by appearances, Zazu," Simba told him. "Not all of us can be as handsome, or as intelligent, or as cultured as yourself, for instance."

"Oh, I say, Sire, do you really think so?"

Zazu started to preen his feathers and then remembered the matter in hand.

"Sire, this creature was unlike any rhinoceros I've seen before. For one thing it was uglier and blacker than any other rhino I've ever seen, and with a horn so sharp and nasty it could skewer a baby elephant. I tell you, Sire, I've never seen its like before."

"Hmm..." Simba remembered the tales his father had told him when he had been a young lion cub.

Once, so Mufasa had said, there were two great families of rhino who roamed the plains of Africa. The black rhino was by far the nobler of the two. However, year by year, their numbers shrank. Soon, so some said, there would be none left at all.

When Simba had asked his father why the black rhino were disappearing, Mufasa had bowed his head in sadness. Then he had looked over to the horizon, to those shadowy places which were forbidden to members of the Pride Lands. There were some things in this world it was better not to know about, he had told his son.

"Let him be, Zazu," Simba advised his old friend. "You may never have seen his type before but he is doing no one any harm."

"But, Sire—" Zazu protested. Simba raised a

paw and told him to be silent.

"We all have to live together," Simba said. "Now go and tell everyone that there is no need to worry. A black rhino is no threat to any of us here in the Pride Lands."

Zazu agreed, and flew off to do the Lion King's bidding. But he was very concerned all the same. That rhinoceros did look very threatening indeed.

Later that day, when the sun was sinking low on the horizon, bathing the plain in its warm and rosy glow, Simba was talking to Timon and Pumbaa. They were reminiscing about the old times, before Simba was king, and they had lived and played together in the forest.

Suddenly they heard the sound of hooves, and Timon leapt onto Pumbaa's back.

"Don't worry, old pal!" he cried, as the sound of hooves grew louder and louder. "I'll protect you! If anyone so much as lays a hoof on you then I'll smash them to smithereens!"

Simba smiled at Timon's

attempts to be brave.

"There'll be no need for that," he said, and stood up to greet the two waterbuck who had just arrived, puffing and panting from their long journey.

The waterbuck bowed low before their king, and Simba admired their shiny red coats and handsome horns of the male.

The waterbuck were noble beasts, but unfortunately they smelt, although this was not something which was mentioned in polite circles. If Zazu had been around, Simba would have told him that this also proved that one should never judge by appearances.

Timon held his nose in disgust. "Pheww!" he said. "These guys really stink! You'd think with a name like that they'd have a bath at least once a week!"

By his side, Pumbaa sniffed hard. "I think they smell kind of sweet, Timon," he said, and Timon sighed. It was just his luck to have as a friend someone who was even smellier than a waterbuck!

"Greetings, Kuro and Kanga," Simba said. "What can I do for you?"

"A terrible thing has happened," Kuro panted, trying to get his breath.

"Four waterbuck have been killed down by Kifo River," Kanga said.

"Not just killed," Kuro added, "but slaughtered!"

Timon and Pumbaa looked worried. They didn't like the sound of this at all!

Simba growled. Many animals on the plain killed each other for food. That was part of the great Circle of Life, which everyone knew and respected.

However, no animal killed another just for sport. That was against all the laws of the Pride Lands. Yet, Kuro and Kanga told him that their fellow waterbuck had just been left to die. This was very serious indeed.

Zazu swooped down from out of the sky, and landed at Simba's feet.

"See, Sire, I was right!" he crowed. "The culprit is the rhino I saw this morning at Kifo River. I knew he was a bad sort from the moment I laid eyes on him!"

"Zazu, you have no proof," Simba reminded him.

"A strange animal arrives in the Pride Lands and then waterbuck are killed for sport?" Zazu said. "With respect, Sire, it's too much of a coincidence. Even the most foolish warthog can see that!"

"Yeah," Pumbaa agreed. "That's right – even I can see that! You've got to sort him out, Simba, show him who's boss."

"The future of the Pride Lands is at stake!" Timon agreed.

Simba looked at the two waterbuck, and then

at Zazu, Timon and Pumbaa in turn. It was clear that they were all very scared. But their fear was making them blind to one very important fact.

"Very well," Simba said finally. "I will go down to the Kifo River and confront the rhino."

Zazu flew up into the air and clapped his wings together. "Excellent, Sire!" he squawked.

"And you, Zazu, will come with me," Simba added.

"Me?" Zazu came down to earth with a bump. "But, Sire, it's dark now and I'd be no use in a fight and the rhino's so big and ugly and ... and ... and can't we wait for morning?"

"Zazu, you're not a coward, are you?" Simba smiled.

Zazu sighed. He'd got himself into this mess and it seemed as though there was no way he could get himself out of it now.

"Of course not, Sire," he replied, and then grumbled to himself, "Me and my big beak. Even when I was just a chick in the nest, my mother always said it would get me into the most extraordinary trouble..."

Zazu perched on Simba's head as the Lion King stalked across the plain and through the bushes towards the Kifo River. It was dark now, and the Full Moon in the night sky shone brightly down on them. From far away they could hear all the sounds of the African night: the shrill cries of tree hyraxes, the calls of dik-dik, and the trumpeting of bull elephants.

And before them, half-hidden in the shrubs on the edge of the river, they could see a lumbering black shape: the terrible black rhino.

"Sire, are you sure this is such a wise move, after all?" Zazu whispered nervously, and hid himself in Simba's golden mane.

"Someone is breaking our most sacred laws," Simba said solemnly. "And they must be brought to justice."

"Of course, Sire," Zazu replied. He sounded a little uncertain, as Simba padded silently towards the unsuspecting rhino. As he did so, Zazu peeped out from under Simba's mane.

Zazu expected Simba to pounce on his victim, or, at the very least, give out a blood-chilling roar. After all, Zazu reasoned, that was what lions were supposed to do. Instead, when they were just a few feet away from the rhino, Simba pleasantly wished him a good evening.

"Eh? Who's that? Who's speaking?" the rhino

muttered. He turned around, and peered at Simba and Zazu through narrow and piggy eyes. It was obvious that he was very short-sighted, and couldn't see particularly well.

Zazu gulped. The rhino was even more frightening close up. His face was all wrinkled and warty, and his two horns looked sharp and deadly. The rhino had been munching away at some grass and green shoots still hung from out of the corners of his mouth.

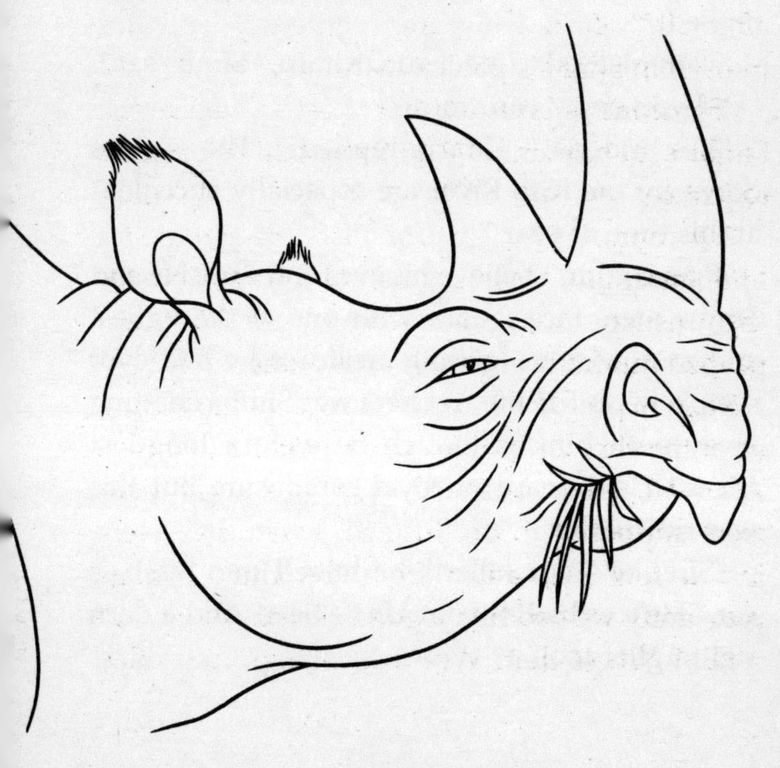

Zazu tugged at Simba's mane, urging him either to attack or, even better, to run away.

"Um, please do excuse me my table manners, Your Majesty," the rhino apologized and gulped down the last of the grass. He swallowed the grass much too fast and gave out an enormous burp. "Most impolite of me, I'm sure!"

Simba laughed and said it didn't matter. He asked the rhino his name.

"Kifaru, if it so pleases Your Majesty," the rhino replied.

"I am pleased to meet you, Kifaru," Simba said. "Did you enjoy your meal?"

"Yes indeed," Kifaru replied. "The shoots down by the Kifo River are especially succulent at this time of year."

Zazu couldn't believe his eyes and ears. He and Simba were face-to-face with one of the ugliest and most vicious-looking creatures he had ever seen in his entire life. Yet here was Simba chatting away with him as though he were a long-lost friend! He'd heard of royal composure but this was ridiculous!

"Sire, he's our killer!" he hissed into Simba's ear. "He's as bad as your Uncle Scar! And a darn sight uglier too!"

Simba shook his head, and Zazu fell out of his mane and landed with a *bump*! right in front of Kifaru. Kifaru looked down at him, and Zazu felt all his feathers go limp with fear. "Kifaru is no killer," Simba told Zazu. He turned back to the black rhino. "Isn't that so, Kifaru?"

"The very idea!" Kifaru said huffily. "Of course I'm not a killer."

"Well, you would say that, wouldn't you?" Zazu said.

"Kifaru is a vegetarian, like all rhinos," Simba said simply.

"Of course, I know that, but..." Then Zazu finally realized what Simba was saying. "That means that he couldn't have killed the waterbuck!"

"Precisely," said Simba. "You weren't thinking straight, Zazu, and you judged Kifaru solely by his appearance. You were frightened of him and so you thought the worst of him."

"Who? Me? Frightened? Never!" Zazu lied, and then turned to Kifaru. "I say, I've made a big mistake, haven't I?"

"Think nothing of it," Kifaru said sarcastically. "It happens all the time. We can't all flit around with our heads in the clouds like you, you know!"

"Well, I've never heard such—" Zazu began, but Simba told him to be silent.

"There is still the matter of who killed the waterbuck for sport," he said. "We must track them down."

Kifaru suddenly twitched his ears. "Quiet!" he said. "I can hear something."

Simba and Zazu fell silent. They knew that the hearing of a rhino is very sensitive indeed.

Sure enough, within a few minutes, two dark shapes approached them. They kept to the shadows, and stayed out of the light of the moon so they wouldn't be seen.

Simba looked down at Zazu. "Zazu, you know what to do," he whispered.

Zazu sighed. "Not again, Sire!" he complained. "When you were a lion cub you used to pounce on me all the time."

Simba grinned. "Aha, but this time I don't

want to use you for pouncing practice!" he said.

"You don't?" Zazu asked. This sounded hopeful.

"Of course not," Simba continued. "This time I want to use you as bait!"

"Well, that's all right then. Wait a minute, did you say *bait*?"

Simba told Zazu to be quiet and pushed him out into the clearing. The full moon shone down like a spotlight on the hornbill. It was impossible for anyone not to see him: he was a perfect target.

"A hornbill like me being used as a sitting duck," Zazu grumbled. "It's just not on!"

The two newcomers stepped out of the cover of shadows and approached the trembling Zazu. They were a pair of hyenas, two of the most ruthless and evil animals ever to roam the grasslands. They licked their lips as they circled Zazu.

"Here's a tasty little titbit for us, eh, Fisi?" one of them said to his companion.

"But Jake we just ate," Fisi said.

"Doesn't matter," Jake said.

"I assure you that you'll find me very tough to eat!" Zazu protested. Jake laughed.

"You can't be much tougher than those waterbuck we nabbed the other day," he said.

"Yuk!" Fisi remembered. "We had to leave them in the end. Still it was fun when they started squealing, wasn't it, Jake?"

"Music to my ears, Fisi, music to my ears!" Jake agreed. "That was a good night's entertainment, that was!"

"You scoundrels!" Zazu said.

"Aw, shut up," Jake said. He stopped as he felt a tap on his shoulder. Jake turned to see Simba smiling at him.

"You should never play with your food," Simba growled.

"Yikes!" Jake exclaimed and dropped Zazu. Zazu landed head first on the ground.

"The table manners of some people!" Zazu complained, and rubbed his aching head.

Simba slashed at the evil Jake with his claws. The cowardly Fisi, instead of helping his friend, turned to run – and found himself facing Kifaru's needle-sharp horn.

"Going somewhere?" Kifaru asked in a deep and threatening voice.

"I suppose this means that dinner's off?" Jake asked as Simba and Kifaru started to advance threateningly on him and Fisi.

"Tonight and for ever!" Simba said, and he and Kifaru raced after the hyenas. Soon they had chased them out of the Pride Lands for good. They knew that they would never return.

"You were marvellous, Sire!" Zazu said when Simba and Kifaru had returned. "And you too, Kifaru. Those hateful hyenas will never come back to the Pride Lands again if they know what's good for them!"

"And the waterbuck are safe again," Simba said. "Zazu, I think you owe Kifaru an apology."

Zazu turned to the rhino. "I apologize for suspecting you, Kifaru," he said, and suddenly felt very ashamed. "I judged by appearances, instead of using my head."

"Just as well I'm thick-skinned enough to take it, then, isn't it?" Kifaru joked, and returned to munching on the grass.

Laughing, Simba and Zazu made their way home.

4

What's Up Croc?

Night had fallen over the Pride Lands, and most of the animals had gone to sleep or had set out on their nightly hunt for food. However, in the shadow of Pride Rock, Zazu, Timon and Pumbaa were very much awake.

Rafiki was telling them stories. The baboon had lived for a long, long time and knew many things that no one else did. For instance, he could tell when the rains were coming from the way the leaves of the acacia tree fell onto the ground. He also knew of the secrets of the elephants' graveyard, of what lay beyond the Pride Lands, and the magic rites which accompanied the birth of the Lion King. Rafiki had been present at the birth of Simba and had presented him to all the creatures of the plain. He was the wisest creature in all the Pride Lands.

Tonight at Pride Rock, however, he was telling his friends ghost stories. Pumbaa shivered as Rafiki spoke of Mambo Croc, the terrible ghost who lurked in the deepest, darkest waters of the Crooked Creek.

"He is the ghost of a mighty crocodile who died many rains ago, and who lays in wait for any unsuspecting passers-by," Rafiki told them solemnly. "And when one is coming by, then he takes them in his mighty jaws, and wrenches them apart limb by limb before swallowing them whole."

Rafiki picked up a twig and snapped it in two, as if to demonstrate his point.

Pumbaa gulped. This worried him a lot, especially as he often went down to Crooked Creek to take a drink. "And this croc guy is still around?" he asked nervously.

"So they say," Rafiki replied, and then smiled gently. "But of course it is just a legend. I don't believe it myself."

Pumbaa breathed a sigh of relief. It looked like he could still go down to Crooked Creek after all!

"You didn't believe that old story, did you, Pumbaa?" Timon sneered, after Rafiki had gone and left them alone.

"Course I didn't," Pumbaa lied.

Zazu stroked his beak thoughtfully. "I don't know though," he said. "There's very often some truth in these old legends. You certainly wouldn't find me flying down to Crooked Creek after dark..."

"Well, I'm not scared of anything or anyone – no way," Timon boasted. "Not like you two snivelling scaredy-cats!"

"I'm not a coward," Zazu said indignantly.

"And I'm not scared either," Pumbaa said. "No ghost of some mangy old crocodile is going to scare me!"

"Oh yeah?" Timon asked his friend. "You'd run faster than an ostrich in a marathon if you ever came face to face with old Croc."

"Wouldn't," said Pumbaa.

"Would," replied Timon.

"Wouldn't!"

"Would!"

Zazu sighed, and flapped his wings. "Will you two stop bickering?" he squawked. "You're as bad as a babble of baby baboons!"

"Well, he said I'm scared," Pumbaa said and started to sulk.

"I bet you wouldn't dare to go to Crooked Creek in the dark," Timon teased.

"Would."

"Wouldn't."

Suddenly a dark shape leapt out from behind a large rock. Startled, Timon shrieked and jumped up onto Pumbaa's back.

"Save me, pal!" he cried out in terror. "It's old Croc come back from the dead to haunt us all!"

Pumbaa turned and started to run. But the newcomer grabbed him by the tail and stopped his escape.

"Pumbaa, why are you running away from me?" asked a familiar voice. The warthog turned around. It wasn't Croc after all, it was Simba!

"Oh, er, hi, Simba," he replied.

Pumbaa now felt very embarrassed indeed. Timon, on the other hand, was jumping up and down with glee on the warthog's back.

"You should have seen your face when you thought old Croc was after you!" he chortled. The meerkat held his sides, he was laughing so much.

"You tricked me!" Pumbaa realized.

"Would someone explain to me what's going on?" Simba asked. He didn't quite understand why Timon was laughing so much, or why Pumbaa was so annoyed.

"Just a touch of high spirits, Sire," Zazu sighed, and told Simba what had been happening. "They are both incorrigibly frivolous!"

"I *am* brave," Pumbaa insisted to Timon.

"You were scared!" Timon chuckled. "Frightened of a ghost story!"

Simba padded up to the two squabbling friends.

"Timon, being brave doesn't mean not being frightened," he told the meerkat. "Being brave means being frightened and still doing what you have to do."

"Yeah," Pumbaa agreed.

"You were still frightened though!"

"Wasn't!"

"Was!"

Zazu sighed. "Here we go again!" he said to Simba.

Timon and Pumbaa made it up the very next day. The two of them couldn't stay enemies for long, and they spent most of the following day hunting for grubs in the scrublands.

They found some juicy beetles and termites, as well as a giant millipede which they shared. It was over twelve inches long, and after they had finished it they felt very tired indeed. It had been a long day, and they were both full up.

"I'm tired," Timon said as he lay in the shade of a thorn tree.

"I could do with a drink," Pumbaa said. The sun was low in the sky now, but it was still very hot.

"There's nothing like hunting for your dinner to make you feel thirsty," Timon agreed, and stood up. "Come on, let's go and get a drink."

"I don't know," Pumbaa said. "It'll be dark soon and the nearest waterhole is miles away. Maybe we should get home before the sun goes down."

Timon slapped his pal on the back. "I know where we can get some water from," he said.

"Where?" asked Pumbaa.

"Crooked Creek!" Timon replied.

Pumbaa shook his head. "I'm not really sure about that..." he said.

"C'mon, my best pal, old Croc doesn't really exist!" Timon said. "There's nothing to be scared of!"

Pumbaa looked doubtful. "Are you sure?" he asked.

"Sure I'm sure!" Timon said cheerfully. "Now, come on, Pumbaa, don't be a coward!"

Timon started to lead the way down to Crooked Creek, and Pumbaa followed reluctantly. He wasn't feeling particularly brave and he just hoped that Timon was right about old Croc being nothing more than a legend.

Because if old Croc did put in an appearance,

then Pumbaa knew that he would be away faster than a speeding cheetah chasing after its dinner.

By the time Timon and Pumbaa had reached Crooked Creek, the sun had slipped down below the horizon. It was night now, and it was difficult to see. The moon had been covered by clouds, and it was almost pitch-black.

Tiny fireflies darted to and fro in the air, and Pumbaa snapped at one or two. He was feeling hungry again and the fireflies made a tasty light snack. Timon made his way down to the bank of Crooked Creek. The reeds waved to and fro eerily in the evening breeze, and a strange and spooky mist hung over the waters of the creek.

From far off in the distance there came strange high-pitched squealing sounds. Pumbaa trembled. He knew that the noises he was hearing were probably only the hunting calls of bats, as they searched for food. That didn't help much though; Pumbaa hated bats. As far as he was concerned they were the servants of old Croc, searching out new victims for their master.

He watched Timon, who was strolling down to Crooked Creek as if he hadn't a care in the world. Timon snatched a firefly out of the air and held it

in front of him, using its light to guide him down to the water's edge.

Timon stopped and turned round. "What are you waiting for, Pumbaa?" he asked.

Pumbaa hesitated, and tried to catch a firefly to light his own way down to the creek. The fireflies were too quick for him, however, and he couldn't quite grab hold of one.

"Do you really think this is such a good idea, Timon?" he asked nervously.

"*Hakuna matata* – no worries!" Timon replied nonchalantly. "There's no danger."

"Are you absolutely and a hundred-and-one per cent certain about that?" Pumbaa asked.

"Trust me, Pumbaa!" Timon said. "When have I ever let you down before?"

"Well, there was that time when we wanted a scorpion supper and you asked me to catch one and told me that it wouldn't sting," Pumbaa remembered. "And then there was that time when we were in the jungle and you asked me to cross a river by swinging on a vine hanging from a tree..."

"So?" Timon couldn't quite see what all the fuss was about.

"It wasn't a vine – it was a python," Pumbaa reminded him. "And then there was that time when..."

"All right, all right!" Timon said and told his friend to stop. "But this time you really can trust me, OK?"

Pumbaa followed Timon down to the edge of the creek. The water lapped gently around his feet, and Timon bent down to take a sip.

Suddenly everything went black. Pumbaa looked up nervously in Timon's direction. It was now very dark and it was difficult to see properly.

"What's happened?" Pumbaa asked.

"The firefly's flown out of my hand!" Timon said. His voice was trembling. It sounded to Pumbaa that his best friend was very frightened indeed.

"Well, that's nothing to worry about," Pumbaa said. "Just catch another one, Timon ... Timon?"

There was no reply.

"Timon, where are you?" Pumbaa asked. He

peered into the blackness but there was no sign of his friend.

Suddenly there came a blood-curdling scream, and Pumbaa heard the splashing of water.

"Pumbaa, help me!" Timon called out from the darkness. "He's trying to drag me under the water! Old Croc's come to get me!"

"I don't believe you," Pumbaa said. "You're trying to trick me again."

"No, this time it's for real," Timon said. "Save me, Pumbaa, save me!"

Pumbaa looked this way and that, trying to find Timon. Suddenly the moon came out from behind a cloud and bathed Crooked Creek in light. Pumbaa saw Timon, sitting on a rock and laughing at him.

"Fooled you again!" Timon laughed. "Boy, you were really scared this time, Pumbaa, old pal!"

"Timon, that wasn't funny!" Pumbaa said angrily. "You had me really worried then!"

"Hey, it was just a joke," the meerkat said, and then froze. There was a look of fear on his face. He pointed to the Creek. "Behind you, Pumbaa! Look!"

Pumbaa snorted with contempt. "You're not going to catch me out again!" he said.

"No, Pumbaa, this time it *is* for real!" Timon said. "Look! It's Mambo Croc himself!"

Pumbaa turned and looked in the direction of the Creek. The horrible white skull of a crocodile was slowly emerging from the water. Its jaws opened and a horrible sound came from them.

"This is the voice of Mambo Croc," it said. "I have come for Timon."

Timon grabbed hold of Pumbaa. "Save me, old buddy, save me!" he pleaded. "Don't let him get me!"

Pumbaa was terrified. All the stories about Mambo Croc were true after all! He wanted to run and hide; but he realized he couldn't let Timon down. He raced down to the water's edge and snarled at Croc. He threatened the ghost with his tusks.

"You keep away from Timon, you old Croc, you!" Pumbaa said, trying to sound menacing. "He's my friend, and if you want him, then you'll

have to get past me first!"

"And just who might you be?" Croc asked.

"I'm Pumbaa," Pumbaa replied.

"You are just a warthog," Croc declared, "and I am the great god, Croc, the scourge of the savannah and the demon of the darkest depths!"

"So what?" Pumbaa said. "I'm Pumbaa of the Pride Lands, but Timon is still my best friend and I'll protect him from anyone. Even you!"

"So be it," Croc said. "You are a brave warthog, Pumbaa, and I choose not to fight with you. Not yet anyway..."

And with that Croc vanished beneath the waters of Crooked Creek.

Timon hugged Pumbaa. "My best buddy of them all!" he said gratefully. "You've saved me from Croc. I'm sorry for teasing you and saying you were a coward! I'll never do it again. You're the bravest warthog I've ever known!"

"Hey, it was nothing," Pumbaa said. He couldn't believe that he'd just stood up to Croc like that.

"But weren't you frightened?" Timon asked in amazement.

"Frightened?" Pumbaa said. "Who? Me?"

And then Pumbaa fainted.

After Pumbaa had regained consciousness, and he and Timon had left Crooked Creek, old Croc emerged from the water once again. Underneath the skull was Zazu. He had been wearing the skull like a helmet in order to disguise himself as the crocodile demon. He coughed and spluttered.

"Sire, really this is too much!" he protested. "I'm not a fish or a hippo, you know! I don't know how I kept my breath under water for so long!"

Simba came out from his hiding place in the bushes. "You did well, Zazu," he laughed and congratulated his old friend. "Timon and Pumbaa believe they've met old Croc, and Pumbaa has proved to himself just how brave he really is. Somehow I don't think Timon will call Pumbaa a coward again. He's finally learnt his lesson. And Zazu..."

"Yes, Sire?"

"Let's keep this our little secret shall we!"

5

Trouble at the Lake

If it wasn't one thing, then it was another, Zazu thought grumpily, as he flew over the grasslands and headed towards Pride Rock where Simba, the Lion King was waiting for him. Just when you thought that everything was peaceful and quiet and you could get some well-deserved rest, then something like this happened. He was glad that he was the King's herald; he didn't envy Simba the task he had to perform today.

Simba was waiting for him at Pride Rock, the massive outcrop which overlooked the enormous expanse of the Pride Lands. Simba had inherited the Pride Lands on the death of his father, King Mufasa, and it was now his duty to look after the interests of each and every creature who lived here.

Zazu blinked in the early-morning sun. Down

below he could just make out the figures of Simba, and of Rafiki, the wise old baboon who had known Simba since he had been a lion cub. Zazu swooped down and landed on the rock. He made a deep bow to Simba, and nodded hello to Rafiki.

"Good morning, Zazu," Simba said pleasantly. "Your daily report please."

"The hippos are hopping mad, Sire," the hornbill replied, "and the flamingoes are in a furious flap."

Simba chuckled. "That's hardly news, Zazu," he said.

The hippos and the flamingoes had never got on well together. Hardly a week went by without one side falling out with the other, and usually over a trivial matter.

"This time it's serious, Sire," Zazu continued. "Each side is threatening war on the other!"

Simba suddenly looked interested. This was serious news indeed. The laws of the Pride Lands stated quite firmly that no creature should fight with another creature. It was against the very nature of things.

All life in the Pride Lands was held in a very delicate balance, and an animal only ever killed another animal for food. That was the natural order, that was what was right and proper. For the hippos and the flamingoes to be threatening war on each other meant that something was very much amiss.

Simba exchanged a look with Rafiki. The old baboon looked very worried indeed. He shared Simba's own fears, Simba turned back to Zazu.

"What has happened between the hippos and flamingoes, Zazu?" Simba asked.

"I don't know," Zazu admitted. "But when I

flew over Lake Kidogo, near Maji Falls, they were so annoyed with each other that even the pelicans were keeping well clear – and you know what big mouths the pelicans are. They love the chance of some good gossip!"

"When will the hippos and the flamingoes ever learn to live in peace together?" Simba asked Rafiki. "Sometimes I wish life could be so much simpler."

Rafiki smiled thoughtfully. "Life never is," he told him. "And you are the King. It is your responsibility to make sure that all your subjects live together in harmony."

Simba sighed and thought back to the days of his youth. "When I was a young lion cub I thought that being King would be so much fun," he remembered.

"The life of a King is one of duty, and not one of fun," Rafiki told him sternly. "Yes indeed, your father was the great King Mufasa, and, as his son and heir, you have much power and many privileges that others can only ever dream of. But there is a price to be paid for that power. You must uphold the laws of the Pride Lands. You must be available for your subjects whenever and wherever they need you."

"Rafiki speaks the truth, Sire," Zazu agreed.

"I don't recall either the hippos or the flamingoes saying that they needed my help in their dispute," Simba said, although he knew that both Rafiki and Zazu were right.

"They're both much too proud, Sire," Zazu said.

"Stubborn as well," Rafiki added.

Simba sighed: he knew he had no choice. "Very well," he said. "Let's go and see what all the fuss is about."

Lake Kidogo was one of the most beautiful places in the whole of the Pride Lands, a small silver-and-blue lake near a spectacular waterfall. It had been the favourite watering spot for the hippos for as long as anyone could remember. All through the day these great beasts would play and splash about in the waters, wallowing in the mud at the edge of the lake.

The hippos shared Lake Kidogo with flocks of many different birds – pelicans and avocets, oxpeckers and hammerkops. Some of the birds even perched on the hippos' backs, feeding off the tadpoles and parasites that attached themselves to the hippos' hides.

Yet of all the birdlife that dwelt at Lake Kidogo, by far the most beautiful were the flamingoes. Gracefully balancing on one leg like elegant ballerinas, thousands upon thousands of them lined the shores of the lake, stretching out as far as the eye could see.

As Simba and Zazu approached the lake, Simba reflected on how different the hippos and flamingoes were to each other. The hippos were grumpy and dirty, while the flamingoes seemed to spend most of their lives preening their beautiful pink feathers. No wonder they hardly ever got on with each other.

When they arrived at the lake, Zazu flew into the air and let out a loud squawk, to announce his and Simba's presence to the lake-dwellers. However, the noise of the thousands of chattering flamingoes and big-billed pelicans was too loud for him to be heard.

"Try again, Zazu," Simba suggested.

Zazu tried again, this time much more loudly. Still no one took any notice.

"I'm sorry, Sire," he apologized. "If they'd only stop chattering and gossiping for a second..."

Simba smiled. "Let me try," he said, and walked towards a large rock which stood on the edge of the lake. He climbed to the top of it and then opened his mouth and let out a mighty roar which could be heard throughout the Pride Lands.

This time everyone did take notice. The flamingoes stopped their chattering, all the other birds on the lake stopped their gossiping, and the hippos stopped playing around in the mud and the water. Everyone turned to look at Simba.

"Zazu tells me that there is a dispute down here at Kidogo," Simba announced, as he walked down to the edge of the lake. "Would someone like to tell me about it?"

Suddenly a group of ten grunting and grumbling hippos ran towards Simba and Zazu.

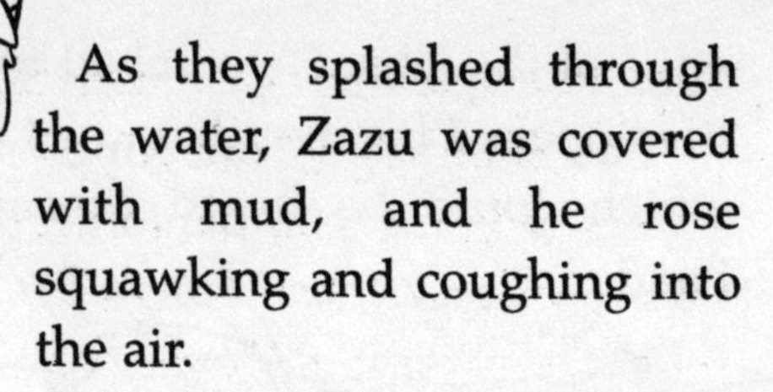

As they splashed through the water, Zazu was covered with mud, and he rose squawking and coughing into the air.

At the same time a flock of flamingoes flew over to Simba, all of them chattering and screeching, as they tried to tell Simba why they had fallen out with the hippos.

The noise was so loud that Simba could hardly hear himself think. He certainly couldn't tell what the flamingoes or hippos were trying to say to him. He roared again, and everyone was silent once more.

"We will discuss your problems at Pride Rock at noon," he commanded.

All at once the hippos and the flamingoes started to move as one in the general direction of Pride Rock.

"Not all of you!" Simba said wearily. "Pick one representative each and send them to me."

The hippos started to talk amongst themselves, wondering which of them could represent them the best. None of the hippos was particularly keen to argue their case with Simba.

"You should go," one hippo said to another.

"Oh, no," his companion replied. "You are so much better at these things."

On the other hand, every one of the flamingoes wanted the chance to show off at the court of the Lion King. They started arguing amongst themselves.

"Let it be me!"

"No, me!"

"Me! Me! Me!"

Simba and Zazu sighed, and started to walk slowly back to Pride Rock. When the hippos and flamingoes finally decided who should represent them, then they would meet them there.

The representatives of the hippos and the flamingoes arrived at Pride Rock at the appointed time. The hippos had chosen the burly down-to-earth Kiboko, while the flamingoes had asked the tall and elegant Yeye. On their arrival at Pride Rock where Simba, Zazu and Rafiki were awaiting them, they bowed before the King.

"Now what's the problem?" Simba asked.

Kiboko and Yeye both started talking at once. Zazu and Rafiki each covered their ears: if the

hippo and the flamingo were going to carry on like this then they'd get no sense out of them at all!

"One at a time, please!" Simba said. He nodded to Kiboko, and told him to speak first.

"Well, Sire, of course it's all the flamingoes' fault," he began in his deep and throaty voice.

"It most definitely is not!" Yeye piped up and fluttered her feathers angrily.

"Yeye, be quiet!" growled Simba. "You will get your chance to speak in a minute. Now, please continue, Kiboko."

"Thank you, Sire," Kiboko said, and gave Yeye

a scornful look. "The flamingoes are irresponsible and never stop partying. All day and all night they're up chattering and squawking, squawking and chattering. We can't get to sleep for all their noise. We've asked them to be quiet, but will they listen? Oh no, not them. Lake Kidogo was a respectable area before they moved in. Now they're bringing down the tone of the whole neighbourhood with their all-day parties!"

"*We're* bringing down the tone of the whole neighbourhood?" Yeye asked in amazement. "You're a fine one to talk!"

"It's always the same," Kiboko grumbled. "The flamingoes spot an underdeveloped area, and before you know it, they move in with all their fancy ideas."

"We're trying to make the place upmarket!" Yeye protested. "Give it a bit of class. Increase the property prices. Heaven knows, it needs it!"

"Yeye!" Simba said, and told the excitable flamingo to be quiet once more. "Is that all you have to say, Kiboko?"

Kiboko nodded. "Yes, Sire," he said.

"Very well," Simba said. "Now, Yeye, what is your side of the story?"

Yeye strutted forwards on her thin and shapely

legs. She tossed her head back and began.

"Would you honestly like the hippos living next door to you, Sire?" she asked and gave Kiboko a look of contempt. "Take Kiboko here. He wallows around in the mud all day, leaving his dirty hoofprints all over the place. The hippos take no pride in their appearance, they're not elegant and refined like we flamingoes. All they do is grunt and eat."

"Unlike you flamingoes, I suppose," Kiboko grunted. "All you do is screech and screech and screech."

Yeye chose to ignore the discontented hippo. "Quite frankly, Sire, when fellow flamingoes from other lakes ask us where we live, we're ashamed to admit that we have such common neighbours," she said.

"And what about your parties, Yeye?" Simba asked. "Are they really as noisy as Kiboko here says they are?"

"They're mere family get-togethers, Sire," Yeye replied. "Just a few thousand of us discussing the finer and more important things of life. We wouldn't expect the hippos to understand that."

"The finer things in life!" Kiboko sneered. "All

they talk about is how wonderful they all are!"

"Well, we are!" Yeye insisted. "Better a graceful, well-bred flamingo than a fat and lumpy hippo! Hippos have no class at all! You all belong in the mud!"

"Better a down-to-earth hippo than a stuck-up and snooty flamingo!" Kiboko retorted.

"Will both of you stop quarrelling for a moment!" Simba growled. Kiboko and Yeye fell silent.

"I've listened to both of you carefully," Simba

said. "And now it is time to give you my judgement."

Kiboko and Yeye looked anxiously at Simba. Which side would he choose to believe?

"Kiboko, you and the other hippos must leave Lake Kidogo," he said finally. Kikobo's face fell. Yeye, on the other hand, squeaked with triumph.

"A wonderful judgement, Your Majesty!" she squealed. "I knew that you would be on our side. After all, you're intelligent, cultured, handsome – and what a party we are going to have tonight!"

"Yeye, do be quiet!" Simba said. "I haven't finished yet!" He turned back to Kiboko who was trying to hold back a tear. Simba smiled sympathetically at him. "Kiboko, after one day you will return to Lake Kidogo. The second day Yeye and the flamingoes will leave the lake for one day only."

"Your Majesty, I don't understand," Kiboko said.

"On the third day you will both see me again at Pride Rock," Simba commanded them. "And then we will decide who Lake Kidogo should belong to."

Simba dismissed Kiboko and Yeye and, after they had gone, he turned back to Zazu and Rafiki who had been watching in silence.

"Well, I think I handled that very well, don't you, Zazu?" Simba asked.

Zazu was confused. "But Sire, all you have done is delayed your decision for a few more days," he said.

Simba shook his head. "It is not me who will make the decision. Kiboko and Yeye will make it," he told the hornbill.

"You'll never get those two to agree on anything," Zazu said.

By his side Rafiki started to laugh. He had guessed exactly what Simba's plan was.

"You've learnt well, Simba," he chuckled. "That really was the judgement of a king!"

Zazu looked first at Simba, then at Rafiki, and asked: "Pardon me for being such a bird brain but would someone please tell me what's going on around here?"

As the third day dawned, Simba and Zazu waited on Pride Rock for Kiboko and Yeye. Presently they arrived as promised. Yeye looked red-eyed and tired. Kiboko was even dirtier than usual and every so often had to pause to scratch himself.

"Well, have you reached a decision?" Simba asked the two of them.

Kiboko and Yeye nodded, and looked sheepishly at Simba.

"We have indeed reached a decision, Sire," Kiboko said.

"And if it's all the same to you, Your Majesty," said Yeye, "we'd like to continue to share Lake Kidogo."

Simba pretended that he was astonished. "Have you made up with each other and reconciled your differences then?"

"Yes, we have," Yeye said.

"And what made you change your mind?" Simba asked.

"Well, when the hippos left on the first day the hyenas and jackals started to show an interest in the lake," Yeye told him. "When the hippos shared the lake with us then they never dared to come so close." She let out an enormous yawn. "None of us got any sleep at all – we all of us had to keep a look-out for them all the time."

Simba smiled. That had been part of his plan. In fact, the flamingoes hadn't been in any danger at all. He had asked Nala and the other lionesses to keep a watchful eye over them while the hippos were away. Of course, he would never tell Yeye that.

Simba turned to Kiboko. The old hippo was obviously very itchy and was scratching himself madly.

"And what made

you change your mind, Kiboko?" he asked.

"Well, Sire, when we returned to Lake Kidogo on the second day and the flamingoes left, then all the other birds flew away in solidarity," he revealed. "Including the oxpeckers and the hammerkops who peck the ticks and parasites off those hard-to-reach places on our backs. We've been so uncomfortable ever since!"

"So you agree to live in peace with each other from now on?" Simba asked.

"Absolutely," Yeye said. "The hippos aren't so bad after all. And it does take all sorts to make a world."

"And the flamingoes have promised to cut down on their partying," Kiboko said. "They might even invite us to their next one."

"Then it's all settled," Simba said, "peace can return to Lake Kidogo."

Kiboko and Yeye said their goodbyes and walked off back to their lake. When they had gone, Zazu slapped Simba on the back.

"Congratulations, Sire. King Mufasa himself couldn't have done better!" he said. "A masterly display of cat-like cunning and feline foresight if ever I saw one."

"Why thank you, Zazu," Simba said. "I knew

that the hippos and the flamingoes couldn't survive without each other for long. Each of us is dependent on each other whether we like it or not. We're all part of this great big world, playing our own part in it."

"That's the secret of peace and harmony – that's the secret of the Pride Lands."

Junior Novelisatons

THE LION KING

It is dawn on the African plain, but this is no ordinary day. Today, the grassland animals journey to Pride Rock to see their newborn prince.

As time passes, the young prince Simba grows up into a lively young cub who loves to play with his best friend, a lioness cub called Nala. But Simba's world is not as safe as it seems. His uncle, the evil Scar, wants to be king himself, and will stop at nothing to achieve his goal...

Aladdin

When Aladdin the street rat finds a magical lamp containing an all-powerful genie, it seems that all his wishes can come true. But the Sultan's evil vizier, Jafar, desires the lamp more than anything else in the world, and will go to any lengths to get it back... Aladdin, together with the genie, the magic carpet and his trusty friend Abu, bravely confronts Jafar's evil power, even after he has stolen the lamp and gained control of the Kingdom. Can Aladdin defeat Jafar, win his princess, and free his friend the genie?

The Aristocats live happily in a beautiful mansion in Paris with their mistress, Madame Adelaide. But one day Edgar, the evil butler discovers that the cats are going to inherit all Madame's fortune, and he wants it for himself. So he kidnaps the Aristocats and tries to drown them in the river! Luckily, he hasn't reckoned on Thomas O'Malley and the alleycats...